# My Wish for Christmas!
## The Luke Project

By: Andrea M. Polnaszek, LCSW

# My Wish for Christmas!
## The Luke Project

Written by: Andrea M. Polnaszek, LCSW
Cover Art: Angela Rae Barribeau
Illustrations by: Angela Rae Barribeau
Jennifer Polnaszek
Assistant to Author: Renee Wurzer
Graphic Designer: Lisa Fischer

Copyright © 2015, 2016 Andrea M. Polnaszek
Printed in the United States
ISBN: 978-1-7349123-8-8

## Table of Contents

A Place to Begin .................... 1
Week 1 ................................. 4
Week 2 ................................. 18
Week 3 ................................. 32
Week 4 ................................. 46
Week 5 ................................. 60
Life Code Poster ................. 75
Resources ........................... 78
Scriptures ........................... 79

# A Place to Begin

This little book is intended as a guide through Advent, a preparation for Christmas. It is something you can do by yourself or with a group. If you are like me the holidays are full of commitments, expectations, and there is never enough time for everything. This is not intended to be a burden. Do one day or twenty days, read one sentence or every paragraph. Feel free knowing that whatever time you invest in understanding God's story will make your Christmas celebration that much sweeter.

*This book offers a few different options:*

**Weekly meditation** sets the theme for the week. It is a short summary and background for the daily readings.

**Daily devotion** divides the theme of the week into five readings. The scripture is included so that you can throw this book in your bag and not really need any other tool. This makes it great for the carpool line, unexpected canceled appointment, the gym, or a long line at the grocery store.

**Journaling** is a place each day to reflect. A blank page can be very intimidating. The activity will provide a starting point. It's amazing how when we stop running for a few minutes the stuff in our heads and hearts begins to pour out.

**Something to do each week** provides an activity that will help you put the weekly theme into practice. It also offers you the opportunity to share your journey with your family.

There are no rules. You can read one section a week, a day, skip a few days and catch up or not. This is about spending a little time acknowledging your expectations for Christmas and remembering what the Christmas story is really all about.

# Creativity and Journaling

A few years ago I took a therapeutic journaling class. Many of the other women who took the class were true artists. The journal entry posts they shared were works of art. I appreciate art, but I am busy and I don't have a designated space for art journaling. I have added a few tools to my own journaling experience that make made it fun, expressive, and artistic, even for those of us who are gifted differently.

***Here are some things I like to have:***

- ✓ Colored pencils.
- ✓ Markers in 8-12 colors, too many can be overwhelming.
- ✓ Stickers, like the $1 sticker packs from craft stores tuck neatly inside the journal and can be used to help us feel more artistic or creative.
- ✓ Gel pens in different colors provide a flare for the dramatic when writing simple reflections and journal notes.

# My Wish For Christmas

The word "Christmas" is kinda like "Mufasa." When the hyenas from the Disney movie *The Lion King* heard the king's name they would cackle. Their response both celebrated the king's absence and nervously awaited his return. The holidays can be like that. Christmas can conjure feelings of reverence, excitement, and hope; or fear, stress, and trepidation. How was Christmas last year? Did it meet your expectations, or were you disappointed? Did you enjoy every minute, or watch the minutes tick down on the clock wishing for Christmas to be over?

When I was growing up, I imagined my married life with children to look like a Hallmark Christmas Special. I imagined eggnog sipping at tree-trimming parties where my husband and I wore coordinated outfits. It wasn't too long into my married life when I realized that those expectations were not going to be fulfilled. My husband had no problem with me decorating, preparing, and even planning our holiday celebration, but he didn't really want to participate. In fact every year, a few weeks before Christmas, my husband would go into a seasonal malaise. It wasn't difficult to understand since he had lost his father on Christmas morning and that very weekend marked the beginning of the end of his first marriage. Christmas was a tough time for him. His struggle with the season required me to change my expectations. I was left with the reality that my dream for us as a Christmas couple was not going to be realized.

Advent is traditionally a time when we focus on the idea of hope. Part of that process requires reflection about where we are. Where is the place you find yourself? What is your Christmas baggage? What memory do you have that steals your Christmas joy? Over the next few weeks spend a little time thinking about the hurts that have stuck and the disappointments that stand in the way of joyfully experiencing the celebration of Jesus' birth this year.

# Meditation: Hope

The first week is recognized as the week of HOPE. Church goers celebrate the hope of a coming Savior. Most of the West recognizes a long Christmas to do list that includes: gifts, parties, and family gatherings. We are transfixed by marketers that sell us a cup of coffee and a lifetime of dreams. For some of us the Folger's® commercial embodies Christmas reality. For the rest of us, it is a fantasy story: a Christmas dream that has never really come true. So, this Christmas we have hope that maybe the Folger's® commercial will happen for us. We have hope!

Does Christmas actually produce a large lump in your throat and a tightness in your belly? If so, you are not alone. It does the same thing for me. I have enjoyed a lot of fun. I have a few of those perfect Christmases when I made cookies, cleaned the house, and hosted our holiday party. There were also years where we had family fights, not enough resources for the American Christmas dream, and I only unpacked one box of Christmas decorations.

One year my daughters asked: "How come we don't put up outdoor Christmas lights?"

My husband and I stared at each other realizing we had become tired and just not done it! If you are dreading some parts of Christmas, you are not alone.

Hope in itself is a good thing. The celebration of Christmas in its pure form is all about hope. It is the expectation of something good, something better for the future. In ancient times the people were waiting for a Savior, a Redeemer, someone to bring an end to their suffering. I think we are all looking for that as well. Sometimes we mix up the commercial Christmas for the real Christmas. There were no Christmas cards when Jesus was born, instead there was a star. There were no fancy dresses, instead there were dirty shepherds. There were no decorations, instead there were weary parents and a simple manger.

What there was in Bethlehem was hope. New birth brought hope for a new future.

## TO DO THIS WEEK:

Give yourself some space to breath. Allow yourself to be real and acknowledge what is most important about Christmas for you. Make a list of the things you love and make a point to fit them into the coming weeks (even if it is only one thing from the list). Bring the hope back to Christmas by feeding your spirit. Invite your family to watch ***A Charlie Brown Christmas*** with you. Enjoy!

# Week 1, Day 1

### Dreaming of a Different Day—Barren

*In the time of Herod king of Judea there was a priest named Zechariah, who belonged to the priestly division of Abijah; his wife Elizabeth was also a descendant of Aaron. Both of them were righteous in the sight of God, observing all the Lord's commands and decrees blamelessly. But they were childless because Elizabeth was not able to conceive, and they were both very old. – Luke 1: 5-7*

The story opens with Elizabeth and Zechariah, a childless couple who follow God's ways to the letter of the law. Zachariah is a high priest working at the temple. He spends his days praying and conducting priestly duties, like lighting candles. Elizabeth is from the family line of Aaron. Yes, Aaron, the brother of Moses—the "let my people go" guy. They are both from good stock.

In ancient times barrenness was next to godlessness. This **New Testament** story is recorded before the New Covenant. The Jewish God followers are obeying the Ten Commandments. Zechariah and Elizabeth are following all the "dos and don'ts" blamelessly and still cannot have a baby.

Some of the most highly respected women of the Bible were barren, meaning the family line would stop with them. If you feel like you are praying to no avail, don't give up! The answer may come when you least expect it, in the most miraculous way.

---

Have you ever prayed for something that didn't happen? Have you ever felt barren, asking for something, trusting God and obeying Him as best you can, and still not receiving the gift you desired?

# WEEK 1, DAY 2

### *Receiving a Message*

*Once when Zechariah's division was on duty and he was serving as priest before God, he was chosen by lot, according to the custom of the priesthood, to go into the temple of the Lord and burn incense. And when the time for the burning of incense came, all the assembled worshipers were praying outside. – Luke 1:8-10*

Have you ever prepared long and hard for something and had only one shot at it? It could be the championship game, an audition, a work presentation, or a public performance. Zechariah had spent his life being a priest. He had prayed outside the Holy of Holies day after day, month after month, and year after year. Then one day he drew the right straw. He was charged to enter the Holy of Holies and burn incense.

Zechariah was faithful. He obeyed God. He was blameless in God's sight obeying all His commands. And finally after years of service, in the twilight of his life, it was time. He would get as close to God as possible at that time. He entered God's presence. What a miracle. What an honor. What an occasion.

We live in the light of the **New Testament** where we can talk to God anytime, anywhere, and any way. The Holy Spirit is our advocate making a way for the Holy of Holies to be the bathroom, the living room, or the car. The Holy of Holies is our heart. Thank God for the gift of His presence.

---

Where is your favorite place to spend time with God?

# Week 1, Day 3

### *Fearing and Questioning*

*Then an angel of the Lord appeared to him, standing at the right side of the altar of incense. When Zechariah saw him, he was startled and was gripped with fear. But the angel said to him: "Do not be afraid, Zechariah; your prayer has been heard. Your wife Elizabeth will bear you a son, and you are to call him John." – Luke 1:11-13*

Angels are formidable beings, large creatures, encompassed with light. They are said to be surrounded by the glory of God. Throughout the Biblical narrative the angels comfort their hearers after their arrival with words like: "Don't be afraid."

It would be natural for Zechariah to be in awe, or to fear the creature that stood before him. It would be even more natural for him to ask questions like: "How can this be?"

Zechariah did both of these things. He was struck with awe by the sight of Gabriel and questioned how the things Gabriel was saying could possibly come true.

Zechariah was old and I'm sure he thought it was preposterous that he and Elizabeth could have a baby. The angel was recounting the miraculous. He was telling Zechariah that not only would his dream of being a father come true but that his son would make a way for the coming King. The very entity that Zechariah had studied, worshiped, and led others to follow would be coming soon. His own son would prophesy of the coming Savior of Israel and the world.

Zechariah asks: "How can you be sure?"

Gabriel responds: "Because I hang out with God and He told me."

Gabriel concludes by saying: "Because you question my authority you will be silenced for a time until your boy is born."

---

What do modern day angels look like?
What kind of sign do you need to believe that God is coming?

# Week 1, Day 4

### *Watching It All!*

> *Meanwhile, the people were waiting for Zechariah and wondering why he stayed so long in the temple. When he came out, he could not speak to them. They realized he had seen a vision in the temple, for he kept making signs to them but remained unable to speak. – Luke 1:21-22*

There were probably eight thousand worshipers assembled outside to pray while Zechariah went inside the Holy of Holies. It was customary to tie a rope around the priest's leg. Temple officials feared that when a priest came face to face with God, the man might keel over and die. Since only the high priests could go into the sacred space, the temple servants needed a way to get a dead priest out. Hence, they planned to yank on the rope and pull him out.

I wonder if the on-lookers were discussing when to pull on the rope? Zechariah was taking a long time in there. Had he seen God and died, or was God telling him something?

These traditions all point to a realization that the One True God, Creator of the Universe is awe inspiring and powerful. The traditional worshipers believed in the miraculous. They were assembled praying for the unimaginable. Their prayers set the stage for their hearts to witness the miraculous in Zechariah. When high priest Zechariah exited the most holy space he was speechless. And the people knew something had happened.

---

What is God saying to you this Christmas season?
Where is God inviting you to be quiet?

# Week 1, Day 5

### *Finishing Well*

*When his time of service was completed, he returned home. After this his wife Elizabeth became pregnant and for five months remained in seclusion. "The Lord has done this for me," she said. "In these days he has shown his favor and taken away my disgrace among the people." – Luke 1:23-25*

Zechariah finished his priestly duties and returned as usual, back to his sleeper community to do his regular job. He also returned to Elizabeth his wife. And he had news. Big news! They were going to have a baby in their old age. God had spoken. Their son would make a way for the Lord.

After something amazing happens, I can't wait to text or call my husband. Sometimes I don't even make it into the car before I send him a message with my news. Zechariah did it differently. He didn't run out of the temple to be with his wife after the angel talked to him. He didn't hurry the process of making the baby. He diligently finished what God had instructed, and when it was his appointed time to leave, he went home to share the news and consummate their relationship.

Finishing well is a valuable, Godly concept. The end is as important as the beginning. I once heard someone say: "You are really good at beginnings, not so good at endings."

God is a God of Fulfillment. He promises to complete what He has begun. As His followers, we are to walk in His ways. Just like Zechariah we are to end things well—as much as it is up to us!

We leave Zechariah and Elizabeth enjoying quiet celebration of God's favor, a baby!

---

What do you need to wrap up?
What have you left hanging at work, with family or friends?
Where do you need to move backward before you move forward into this Christmas season?

# Week 2

## Prepare - The People We Are Becoming

# Meditation: Prepare

The second week is commonly recognized as the week of PREPARATION. The ancient story records the steps that Mary and Joseph made to get to Bethlehem. They were fulfilling the expectations of the kingdom by registering in Joseph's city of birth, Bethlehem. In this second week we prepare by buying gifts, wrapping presents, hanging decorations, and so much more. Sometimes those very preparations can cause us to feel frustrated, resentful, and exhausted.

Preparing means to "get ready." You may be thinking "I don't want to get ready" for a repeat of our last Christmas season. So, let's get ready for something new!

What would it look like if you took back Christmas? What if you prepare for the things you love and don't do the things you resent? What if you invited your family to make a list of their top three favorite parts of Christmas and you made a plan to make that happen? Even if you don't all agree, everyone gets to celebrate one tradition that is important to them. What if celebrating with a family member in their favorite tradition became the gift, rather than a source of resentment? The little gifts you give are steps of preparation in this Christmas season.

# To Do This Week

Place a glass jar in a prominent place: the counter, kitchen table, or next to the coffee pot. Put a small pad of paper or stack of note cards next to it. Encourage your family members to write down their top three favorite holiday traditions. Then go through them one by one as a family, walking down memory lane and enjoying each other's favorites. Or, take the slips of paper and make a master list. Consider how to plan including these traditions into the next three weeks.

# WEEK 2, DAY 1

### *Seeing an Angel*

*In the sixth month of Elizabeth's pregnancy, God sent the angel Gabriel to Nazareth, a town in Galilee, to a virgin pledged to be married to a man named Joseph, a descendant of David. The virgin's name was Mary. The angel went to her and said, "Greetings, you who are highly favored! The Lord is with you." – Luke 1:26-28*

God sent the same angel. He sent Gabriel to tell Mary that she was favored and chosen by God to bring Jesus into the world. Mary is troubled but she does not seem alarmed. One conclusion is that she has studied the **Torah**, that she has walked closely with God. She is expecting a Savior.

I find this exchange comical. The angel says: "Greetings." He says "Hi."

It makes me wonder what Mary was doing. Was she washing the laundry, or grinding wheat into flour? Was she making the bed, or folding towels?

The angel appears and says "Hi, God has found delight in you."

In other words, God has been watching from the heavenly realms and has chosen a young lady by the name of Mary to bring His Son earthly life.

Then Gabriel says: "The Lord is with you!"

From my vantage point I wonder if Mary would think: "God better be. I have been following Your laws God. I've been waiting for Your Messiah to come and now You have chosen to bring God with skin-on into my neighborhood, into my upcoming marriage, into my life. Thanks Gabriel. God better be with me."

It's not enough that Mary would see an angel. That alone is a miracle. But, the angel also talked to her and gave her directions straight from the mouth of God.

---

What is God asking you to do that is bigger than you?
How has God found favor with you?
Is the Lord with you?

# Week 2, Day 2

### *Fearing, Yet Believing*

> *Mary was greatly troubled at his words and wondered what kind of greeting this might be. But the angel said to her, "Do not be afraid, Mary; you have found favor with God. You will conceive and give birth to a son, and you are to call him Jesus. He will be great and will be called the Son of the Most High. The Lord God will give him the throne of his father David, and he will reign over Jacob's descendants forever; his kingdom will never end." – Luke 1:29-33*

This is a troubling message. So much of what Mary is being told was foretold. She knows what the **Torah** says. She has been waiting for one like David to redeem her people. She and her people have been waiting for the Kingdom that will never end, ruled by God and not by tyrannical dictators like Herod.

Mary is troubled. She is probably confused. After all, the Israelites had not heard from God in over 400 years. Gabriel's announcement comes after a long silence and years of blind faith. Mary may have wondered about the mysterious greeting. She may have wondered what it meant to be favored by God.

Well, Gabriel doesn't mince words. He instructs her to not be afraid. These are words of comfort followed by a message that would have struck fear in my heart. He says: "Don't be afraid because God has chosen you to give birth to a son. He wants you to name Him Jesus; He is the Son of the Most High."

This is a miracle with crazy consequences. She is pledged to be married to a man. The story insinuates that they were not married and therefore would not have had sexual relations yet. This is news that could be considered a curse. And Mary is told: "Don't be afraid."

---

What is the last time fear struck your heart?
How did you deal with it?
In what ways did God provide an angel to comfort you?

# WEEK 2, DAY 3

## *Wondering*

*"How will this be," Mary asked the angel, "since I am a virgin?" The angel answered, "The Holy Spirit will come on you, and the power of the Most High will overshadow you. So the holy one to be born will be called the Son of God. Even Elizabeth your relative is going to have a child in her old age, and she who was said to be unable to conceive is in her sixth month. For no word from God will ever fail." – Luke 1:34-37*

Mary simply wonders: "How, because I am a virgin?" She is confused by the particulars. Then the angel brings width and depth to her wondering. He says: "The Holy Spirit will be upon you and the Most High will overshadow you."

N.T. Wright brings the best insight I have found on this question: "The angel gives a double explanation for the whole event. The **Holy Spirit** will come upon Mary, enabling her (as the Spirit always does) to do and be more than she could by herself. But at the same time 'the power of the Most High' will overshadow her. This is something different: God himself, the creator, will surround her completely with his sovereign power." *– Luke for Everyone, page 10.*

The angel's answer to Mary's wondering is incredible. He simply tells her that God in Spirit and as the Father will allow her to do more, be more, and experience a miracle in, through, by and for God Himself. This is an amazing little piece of scripture. The angel's speech ends with a message of companionship: "You are not alone; your relative has been touched by God as well." And the final thought: "For no word from God will ever fail." A more familiar translation says it like this: "Nothing ... is impossible with God."

Invite God to fill you and allow you to do far more than you could ask or think.

---

What is on your too impossible for God list?
Who has God provided for you to walk with on this journey?

# Week 2, Day 4

## *Obeying*

> *"I am the Lord's servant," Mary answered. "May your word to me be fulfilled." Then the angel left her.* – Luke 1:38

So the angel arrives while Mary is doing the dishes. He says she has found favor with God. He instructs her not to be afraid. He explains what is going to happen. He tells her about her cousin Elizabeth. He finishes up by saying: "Nothing is impossible with God."

And Mary responds eloquently: "I am the Lord's servant."

Remember that Mary has followed God in the Jewish tradition. She has learned and followed the law. She is expecting a Savior.

In this exchange, Gabriel uses familiar jargon like "The Most High." She knows this is the God who she serves.

When the angel—THE ANGEL—reassures her with more instructions of what is to come she says: "I am the Lord's servant." Wow!

The **New Living Translation** says: "I am your servant girl."

This is what Mary was taught from the time she was knee high. And in the face of meeting an angel, she is so in tune with God and His covenant that she assumes a servant's posture and says: "May your word to me be fulfilled."

In other words she says: "OK, bring it on!"

---

This Christmas, how is God providing you space to be a servant?
Where can you respond like Mary? "May all you have said be fulfilled."

# Week 2, Day 5

### *Preparing*

*At that time Mary got ready and hurried to a town in the hill country of Judea, where she entered Zechariah's home and greeted Elizabeth. – Luke 1:39-40*

The scripture doesn't say that Mary tells her mom. She doesn't stop to tell Joseph or her neighbors. She quickly packs her things and leaves. She hurries to visit her cousin Elizabeth.

Have you ever shared something incredible or miraculous with someone who just didn't get it? You told a friend, a family member, or your spouse about something special and they just didn't get it. They may have said something like: "I remember when that happened to me." And as you listen to their reflection of your story something in your gut just says: "No, you don't get it!"

Mary goes straight into see Elizabeth. It almost seems like she doesn't knock. I imagine her clamoring for the door knob and pushing her way into the house, desperate to see the face of someone who will understand.

Mary just received preposterous news. She has believed and accepted the mission from God. The angel left her with word that her cousin, the one who had wanted a baby her whole married life, could relate. Elizabeth—the woman people snickered at and laughed at during family gatherings because she was barren—Elizabeth was pregnant.

There must have been a knowing. Maybe it was a gleam in Gabriel's eye since he had brought the news to Zechariah some months before, a knowing that Mary needed to connect with one who would understand. How good God is to give us family and friends who can share the unbelievable with us!

---

Whose house can you walk into without knocking?
What can you do with them to celebrate Christmas this year?
What is your unbelievable? Who was there when it happened?

# **MEDITATION: JOY**

The third week is commonly recognized as the week of JOY. The **Merriam-Webster** dictionary defines joy as "a feeling of great happiness." I like to think of joy as that all over good feeling from the top of my head to the tips of my toes. I like to think of joy as lite and light. The Christmas season is full of lights. We put lights on the outside of our houses. We put lights on our trees. But what about the light in us?

The first Christmas was full of light. There was the angel Gabriel who came to the shepherds. He told them that the Savior had come to redeem the world. He invited them to go and see.

The sky was lit up with many angels as they sang and directed the shepherds to Bethlehem. Gabriel promised the shepherds would know they were in the right spot when they found a baby lying in a manger.

We honor the tradition of the first Christmas by hanging lights. We often put stars at the top of our Christmas trees to remember that star that showed the Magi, the Wise Men, where to go (Matthew 2:1-12).

Sometimes celebrating the holidays is as far from joyful as we could imagine. It is full of bad memories, disappointment from broken promises and unfulfilled expectations. Unfortunately there is not much we can do about the past. We can remember it, we can honor it, and we can be real about it but we can't change it. The only moment we have is right now. The only light we have is the light inside us.

What turns on your light? What brings you joy? Instead of doing the same thing and expecting different results this Christmas, do something different. The only thing you can control in any given situation is you. Think of something that brings you joy and turn your light on by doing it.

I find great joy watching Christmas lights twinkle. In the past I haven't had time, energy, or resources to decorate our entire house, so I hung Christmas lights—one strand from a "dollar" store—in my kitchen. After dinner I would turn off the overhead lights and turn on my strand of

Christmas lights. Sitting there with my cup of coffee or tea, I found joy, peace, and enjoyed a little Christmas.

## TO DO THIS WEEK

Find some Christmas lights either in your house or out your window. Boil a cup of tea or pour a cup of coffee and sit watching the lights until your cup is empty. This simple act may just fill up your emotional cup.

Christmas

# Week 3, Day 1

### *Jumping for Joy*

> *When Elizabeth heard Mary's greeting, the baby leaped in her womb, and Elizabeth was filled with the Holy Spirit. In a loud voice she exclaimed: "Blessed are you among women, and blessed is the child you will bear!"* – Luke 1:41-42

Mary arrives to tell Elizabeth that she will have a baby. Not just a baby, but God's Own Son. I imagine that in the days before her pregnancy, Elizabeth might have been discontent. This great news could have been overshadowed by her shame. Baby Jesus may have been a big honking reminder of what Elizabeth did not have—a baby of her own.

Now fast forward. Elizabeth is six months pregnant which means that she has more than a verbal promise of a baby. She has evidence. She looks pregnant. She feels pregnant. And when Mary barges into the house, Elizabeth's baby jumps.

There is no resentment, anger, or contempt for Mary. Elizabeth is in the middle of her own miracle and she can genuinely say: "Blessed are you among women."

Isn't our God good! He gives Elizabeth an awesome responsibility to give birth in her old age to a baby, a son who will prophesy of the coming Messiah. She is given the honor of celebrating with Mary and resonates on a level no one else could—remembering the stories of old like the story of Sarah's miracle baby, Isaac, and her laughter at the word of his coming (Genesis 18:1-15, 21:1-7).

John jumps for joy in Elizabeth's womb. The excitement is palpable. Christ will change everything for a people who have believed.

---

What does joy look like for you?
When is the last time you jumped for joy?
What were you celebrating?
Who did you share it with?

To touch their harps of gold;  
O'er all the wea-ry world;

2. Still through the clov-en sk...

men, From heav-en's all-gracious King":  
plain. They bend on hov-ering wing,

The world in so-lemn still-n...  
And ex-cr o'er its Ba-...

To touch their harps of gold:  
O'er all the wea-ry world;

1. It came up-on the  
2. Still through the clov-e...

is now De-sire

sang cre-a-tio...

Christmas

us, Thee,

# Week 3, Day 2

### *Finding Favor*

*"But why am I so favored, that the mother of my Lord should come to me? As soon as the sound of your greeting reached my ears, the baby in my womb leaped for joy. Blessed is she who has believed that the Lord would fulfill his promises to her!" – Luke 1:43-45*

This entire experience was life changing for Elizabeth. She had been barren for her entire marriage. The townspeople whispered about her. They wondered what she had done to anger God so He would curse her with childlessness. She understands some of the feelings of being an outcast, not included, different.

Elizabeth's words are beautiful. She exclaims: "Why am I so favored?"

She knows what it feels like not to be favored, so when Mary arrives with her news and Elizabeth's baby responds by leaping for joy, Elizabeth knows that something special is happening. She knows Mary is a friend of God. He has shown her great mercy by moving mountains in her life, working a miracle for her family, and now her lineage will be the mother of the promised Savior.

Elizabeth doesn't just leave it at acknowledging Mary's favor; she also validates Mary's faith. She says: "Blessed is she who believed."

Elizabeth knows a little bit about belief. Her own husband had questioned Gabriel, his shock and awe had translated to fear and disbelief. Zechariah's reaction had left him speechless. Surely by now six months into the pregnancy Elizabeth had heard the whole story. Whether by signing or scribbling sentences, her husband had told her what happened. So no wonder Elizabeth is impressed with Mary's faithfulness. And she uses her words to express it.

---

How has God found favor with you?
How has God been faithful to you?
Write a few words of gratitude to thank God for His steadfast love for you.

# Week 3, Day 3

### *Discovering Mercy*

*When it was time for Elizabeth to have her baby, she gave birth to a son. Her neighbors and relatives heard that the Lord had shown her great mercy, and they shared her joy. – Luke 1:57-58*

Mercy is "compassion or forgiveness shown toward someone whom it is within one's power to punish or harm." ***Oxford Dictionary***.

When Elizabeth gives birth to John her neighbors quickly hear about it. First of all, God has given her a son. In ancient tradition there was nothing better. A son meant the family name continued. A son brought honor to the home. And second, God has given her a child after years of childlessness. God's mercy is wrapped in the compassion of the gift of this little boy.

Elizabeth's neighbors and relatives realize the gravity of this baby's birth. They live in the real world and they understand the social-political significance of this act. The neighbors call it mercy. They are joyful for God's mercy. Our hearts need to be in a humbled, servant-like place to recognize God's mercy. The neighbors are not jealous, they are not self-seeking, instead they are joyful.

Joy is a deep satisfaction that often manifests itself with happy emotions. It is a sense of fulfillment that brings contentment and pleasure. Elizabeth's friends are filled with joy at her fortune. The emotions surrounding joy are mercy, grace, and a deep sense of the compassion of humanity.

---

When is the last time you felt joy for someone else' good fortune?
When is the last time you felt joy for the mercy God has granted you?
How could mercy and joy transform Christmas for you this year?

# Week 3, Day 4

### *Breaking Tradition*

*On the eighth day they came to circumcise the child, and they were going to name him after his father Zechariah, but his mother spoke up and said, "No! He is to be called John." They said to her, "There is no one among your relatives who has that name." – Luke 1:59-61*

It was customary in ancient times for the son to carry on the family name. When Zechariah and Elizabeth's friends and family came over for the circumcision party, they started calling the baby "Little Zech." No one would have thought a thing about it. You can almost imagine Elizabeth running from the kitchen, where she was preparing the party food, and saying: "No! That's not his name."

Can you imagine the in-laws' reaction?

A collective gasp is heard across the room when Elizabeth says: "Call him John!"

Ha, what? No one in our family has that name. What does this name mean? Can you imagine Elizabeth's mother sighing and saying: "She's never done it the way I taught her."

Tradition is the transmission of customs or beliefs from generation to generation. Jewish heritage valued story. They remembered the stories of their ancestors through ritual gatherings and festivals. When Zechariah and Elizabeth called their son John, it parted with the expected and changed the course of history.

---

When have you broken from tradition?
Is there an old Christmas tradition you would like to re-engage or a new Christmas tradition you would like to start?

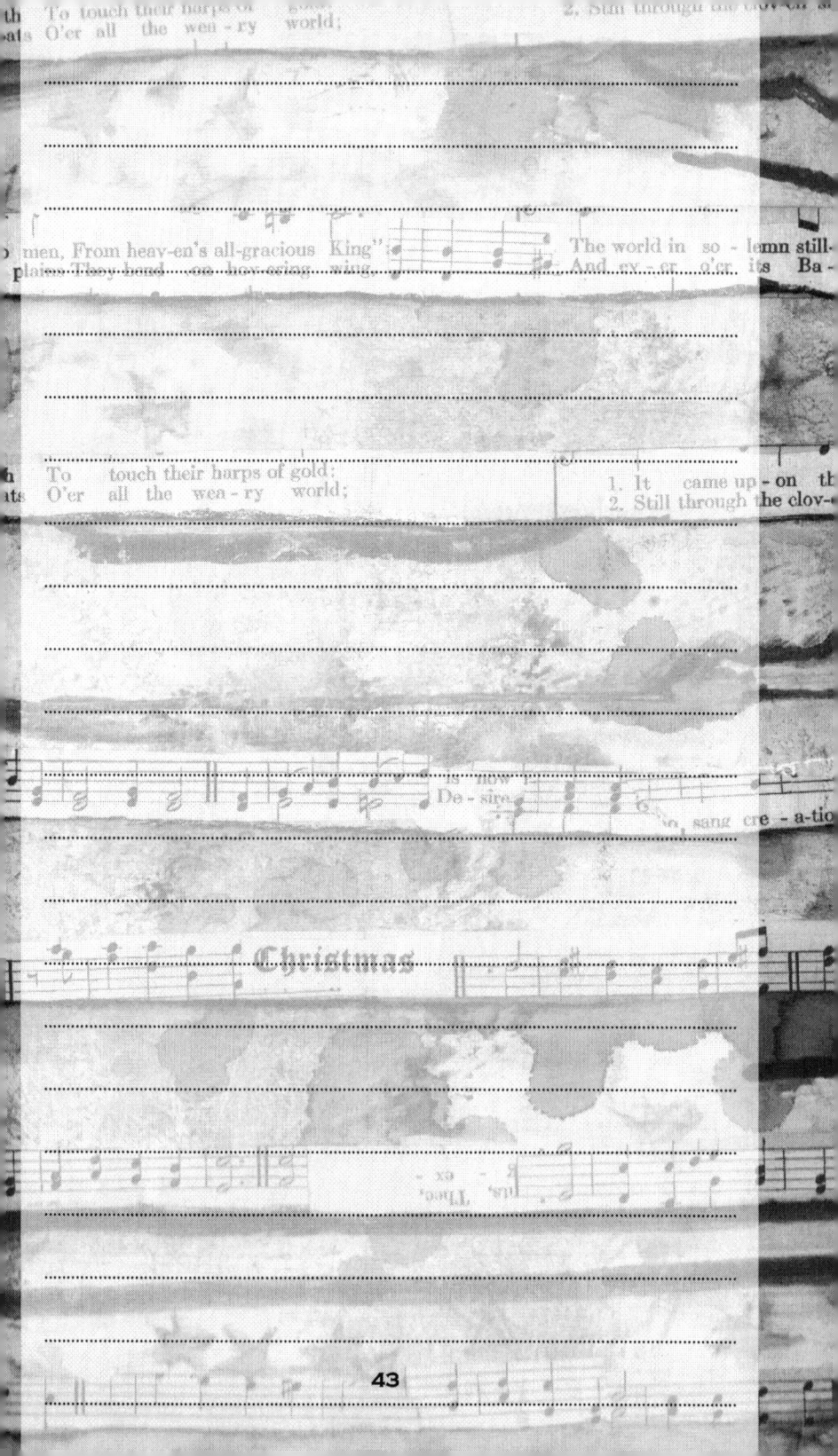

men, From heav-en's all-gracious King" The world in solemn still-
plains They bend on hov-ering wing, And ev-er o'er its Ba-

To touch their harps of gold;
O'er all the wea-ry world; 1. It came up-on th
2. Still through the clov-

De - sire, sang cre - a - tio

Christmas

43

# Week 3, Day 5

### *Finding a Voice*

*Immediately his mouth was opened and his tongue set free, and he began to speak, praising God. All the neighbors were filled with awe, and throughout the hill country of Judea people were talking about all these things. Everyone who heard this wondered about it, asking, "What then is this child going to be?" For the Lord's hand was with him. – Luke 1:64-66*

Zechariah experienced two hundred and seventy days of silence, give or take a few days. He had finished up his service at the temple and returned to be with his wife. They had shared a miraculous pregnancy. Zechariah had followed God his entire life and through this time of quiet he heard the Lord God Almighty's voice in a new way.

Silence had given Zechariah the keen ability to notice everything about Elizabeth's changes. God had plenty of time to remind Zechariah of what was coming. And of course there was plenty of time to review his conversation with Gabriel, over and over and over again.

So, when the traditional circumcision was scheduled and the attendees began to refer to the baby as Zech, he knew this wasn't what God wanted. But he was silent, he could not speak. No one noticed Zechariah's head shaking. It was through the voice of his wife that the party goers turned their attention to him and asked: "What is his name?"

Zechariah reached for his trusty papyrus, the one that had gotten him through the past few hundred days of speechlessness, and wrote: "His name is John!"

The coolest part of this story is that everyone was so overjoyed and amazed at what they experienced that the good news spread all over the place.

---

When is the last time you were quiet before God?
What did He say?

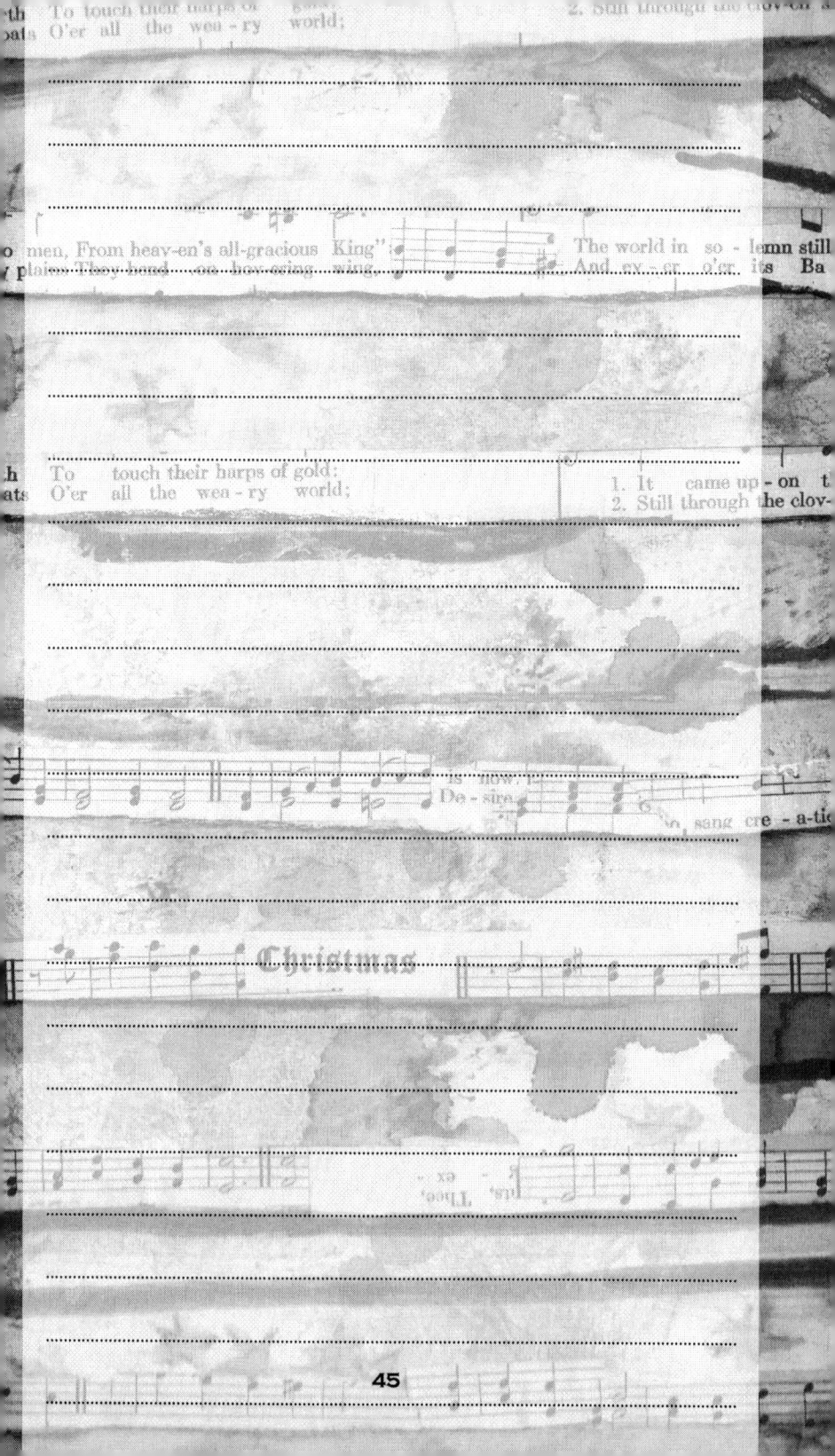

To touch their harps of gold;
O'er all the wea-ry world;

men, From heav-en's all-gracious King"; The world in so-lemn still
plains. They And ex-er o'er its Ba

To touch their harps of gold;
O'er all the wea-ry world;

1. It came up-on t
2. Still through the clov-

De-sire,
sang cre-a-ti

Christmas

Thee, ex

# Week 4

## Love - The Way We Live Our Lives

# Meditation: Love

After all the waiting and expectation Christmas week is finally here. This fourth week is set aside to remember LOVE. Our culture has romanticized love. We have made love about candles, roses, and romance.

Christmas is an opportunity to transform that ideal. Love is celebrated by God sending His Son not to judge the world but to save it. The most loving act we can do is to lay down our life for a friend.

Christmas is the perfect time to see love. We give gifts and appreciate a tiny smile in return. The lights, decorations, and even the tradition of Santa bring life to the mysterious. Love is a noun and a verb. It can mean both the constant affection for a person and the feeling of great affection for a person.

In the midst of the holiday hubbub we can get caught up in the tasks of Christmas and miss the love. Love is an invitation to express and experience great affection for each other. Don't let Christmas go by without opening your heart to some love.

# To Do This Week

This Christmas eve or Christmas day take a time-out from the festivities. Share a note of love for one of your family members or friends. Better yet, look your loved ones in the eyes and tell them about the affection you have for them. This simple act can transform Christmas for you and for someone else.

48

end of eight
Mary
given
Jesus, the
the shepherds
us go over
thing
Lord
they
it is
their own city
child grew and
with wisdom
was upon
41 Now
every
And coming up
she gave thanks to
to all who were
to the law
into Galil
in the law
turtledove
Now the

# WEEK 4, DAY 1

### *Breaking Light Into Dark*

*"... the oath he swore to our father Abraham: to rescue us from the hand of our enemies, and to enable us to serve him without fear in holiness and righteousness before him all our days. And you, my child, will be called a prophet of the Most High; for you will go on before the Lord to prepare the way for him, to give his people the knowledge of salvation through the forgiveness of their sins, because of the tender mercy of our God, by which the rising sun will come to us from heaven to shine on those living in darkness and in the shadow of death, to guide our feet into the path of peace." – Luke 1:73-79*

Zechariah burst into song. He is overwhelmed by grace—the unmerited favor—of God. His first spoken words in months are expressions of thanksgiving to God for delivering His people. He speaks with deep gratitude for the boy—his boy—who will make a way for the Lord.

Notice the rich language Zechariah uses. He is a priest after all and he has much of the holy books memorized. We hear remnants of David's famous Psalm 23 when he says: "the light will break forth on those living in the shadow of death."

Zechariah celebrates that heaven shines on him and us bringing light into dark places where death has cast a shadow. That light remains today, bouncing rays of color into our dark spaces. My favorite part of Zechariah's song, is: "to guide our feet into the path of peace." Later on in the **New Testament** when the armor of God is described, we are encouraged to "put on the shoes of peace." This is a challenge and encouragement to walk into every situation with a spirit of peace. Zechariah is celebrating that his long awaited son has the awesome job of making a way for the Redeemer of the world and that very act will guide God's people on a path of peace.

---

Where do you need a little peace?
What would it look like for you to wear "shoes of peace" wherever you go?
What would peace look like for you this Christmas?

51

# Week 4, Day 2

### *Delivering God*

> *So Joseph also went up from the town of Nazareth in Galilee to Judea, to Bethlehem the town of David, because he belonged to the house and line of David. He went there to register with Mary, who was pledged to be married to him and was expecting a child. While they were there, the time came for the baby to be born, and she gave birth to her firstborn, a son. She wrapped him in cloths and placed him in a manger, because there was no guest room available for them. – Luke 2:4-7*

This is a familiar story. This is actually the crux of Christmas. Christ was born in Bethlehem to Mary, a virgin, and her betrothed Joseph. Scripture says that this was the first census since Quirinius was Governor of Syria. The reason that Joseph and Mary are traveling is to follow the law and be counted. They find themselves in Bethlehem because Joseph was from the family line of David.

All of the prophesy that led up to the birth of John the Baptist heralded that the Redeemer, the King of Israel would come from the line of David. So, as God would have it, Joseph is counted as part of the line of David in the census taken by Quirinius. It is the fulfillment of scripture. A non-internet culture would need such a census to trace lineage and verify connection. The very act of being counted brought further credibility to the Prince of Peace. It is important because Mary would have known all of this rich tradition and the promise of God's law fulfilled through His Son.

I wonder if Mary expected her baby to be born in an overflow room? The inn in ancient times would have had a special area for the animals. It may have been attached to the inn and no doubt it was rustic. In fact the story says that Jesus was laid in an animal feeding trough, a manger. Baby Jesus rests in space set up for weary traveling animals to be fed and bedded before embarking on another journey.

---

What is God reminding you of this Christmas?
How are you making space for Christmas this year?

# Week 4, Day 3

### Seeing the Extraordinary

*And there were shepherds living out in the fields nearby, keeping watch over their flocks at night. An angel of the Lord appeared to them, and the glory of the Lord shone around them, and they were terrified. But the angel said to them, "Do not be afraid. I bring you good news that will cause great joy for all the people. Today in the town of David a Savior has been born to you; he is the Messiah, the Lord." – Luke 2:8-11*

Are you wondering why you remember this part of the story so clearly? After you read: "And there were shepherds living in the fields…" did your memory kick in? I bet you finished the sentences without even reading them. The lovable Peanuts character, Linus, brought these words to life. He stood on the stage of Charlie Brown's disastrous Christmas pageant and recited Luke 2. The sentences flow with more and more confidence when he drops his blanket and proclaims: "Do not be afraid."

This passage is the third time Luke reports the words of the angel: "Do not be afraid." This is an incredible command and invitation. The shepherds are doing their job, tending the sheep out away from town. They are the janitors and housekeepers of their day and age. They are invisible or worse, scorned for their work. And yet God goes to them first. He sends them a brilliant message in the sky.

Shepherds know their sheep. Each sheep knows their shepherd's voice. The sheep listen and follow. What a beautiful image, the lowly shepherds receiving a message from the angels that the Lamb of God has arrived. Just like the sheep know their master's voice, these shepherds knew the voice of their Master and were invited to know the Prince of Peace.

---

What do you follow?
What does the voice of God sound like to you?

55

# WEEK 4, DAY 4

### *Praising in Concert*

*"This will be a sign to you: You will find a baby wrapped in cloths and lying in a manger." Suddenly a great company of the heavenly host appeared with the angel, praising God and saying, "Glory to God in the highest, and on earth peace to those on whom his favor rests." – Luke 2:12-14*

And the angel continues. He tells them where to find the Lamb of God. He will be lying in a manger—a food trough. This is something the shepherds know. They are very familiar with the feeding rituals of animals. The stable is a place where they fit in. The fulfillment will be when the herdsmen see a baby lying in the place where they have traditionally fed their sheep.

After giving these instructions the one angel is joined by many—a heavenly host. The angels are singing, praising, and reiterating the holiness of this moment. The simple song of the angels does three things: acknowledges God's part in this occasion; gives God the glory; and remembers that those who follow are favored and will experience peace.

---

***Take a few moments to do these three things:***

- Acknowledge what God is doing in your life
- Thank God for all He is doing in your life
- Appreciate the favor He has given you

# WEEK 4, DAY 5

### *Obeying the Song*

*When the angels had left them and gone into heaven, the shepherds said to one another, "Let's go to Bethlehem and see this thing that has happened, which the Lord has told us about." So they hurried off and found Mary and Joseph and the baby, who was lying in the manger. – Luke 2:15-16*

Can you imagine it? The music stops and the heavenly light show ceases. All is quiet on the hillside. The shepherds look at each other and they say: "Let's go."

I want to pause here. If this was me and my friends or family sitting out in our backyard witnessing the scene, would I respond this way? On one hand it is easy to suspend our disbelief and say: "Yes. I would be curious."

But before I said: "Let's go," I think my first question would be: "Did you see that? Did anyone else see that?"

The shepherds were trained to care for their flocks. Most would risk themselves for the well-being of their sheep. Their only brush with the miraculous would be through oral tradition. Let's think back to David. God's account says that David was so brave as a shepherd boy that he had killed a lion and bear to protect his sheep (1 Samuel 17:34-36). These amazing herdsmen knew what it was like to have helpless innocent creatures dependent on them. So when angels visit and leave, they are eager to see what has happened.

I wonder if King David—the humble shepherd boy turned king—was their hero? To discover that God had fulfilled His covenant in David's hometown would be intriguing. The shepherds didn't wait; they didn't get rest for the journey. They hurried to look for the feeding trough crib with a baby inside.

---

What have you hurried up to do this week?
Was it worth it?

# Week 5

## Peace - Moving Beyond Christmas

# Meditation: Peace

It's our fifth week and Christmas is over. Did PEACE come to earth in your home this year? Was there goodwill to men after all the toys were unwrapped? If it feels like my home, probably not!

This week is traditionally a time to remember peace. Funny, the unconventional arrival of the Messiah laid in a manger didn't bring political peace as the Jews had hoped. King Herod's wise men were sent to find the "The King" and deliver word back to him so he could have the baby killed (Matthew 2:1-12). There was a threat, danger, and peril.

The emotional hangover from Christmas can feel like Herod's pursuit. Disappointment leads to disconnection and discontent. The idea of peace on earth, goodwill towards men is more than a well wish it is actually a command. Peace is the freedom from disturbance, the presence of tranquility and quiet, engaging in a state of being which is quite active. Goodwill towards others requires us to believe the best in each other, not the worst. Entering into a situation with a spirit of peace can totally transform the outcome. Consider inviting peace into your life this New Year!

# To Do This Week

Make a list of activities and actions that produce peace. Take a step toward peace in your spirit, then do one of the actions on the list for someone else.

62

63

# Week 5, Day 1

### *Spreading the Word*

*When they had seen him, they spread the word concerning what had been told them about this child, and all who heard it were amazed at what the shepherds said to them. But Mary treasured up all these things and pondered them in her heart. The shepherds returned, glorifying and praising God for all the things they had heard and seen, which were just as they had been told. – Luke 2:17-20*

There are so many things that happen in twos or threes in this story. Here again we see the shepherds amazed and jubilant sharing the word about Jesus' birth across the countryside. It must have been brimming out of them because the shepherds were overlooked in their neighborhoods. They were lowly and reclusive but in this story they are telling everyone they know what they have heard and seen. The people are amazed, that means the people are listening.

Mary knows her scripture. She knows where she is in The City of David. She knows what the angel told her. She believes she will be the mother of God's Own Son. She witnesses the shepherds stopping by to affirm her claims. Mary stays quiet. She is a young lady probably around thirteen. She is recently pledged to be married, which is a covenant as strong as marriage in our culture. Joseph is probably older than her. She and he both know this baby isn't his biological son. Mary is human with a divine calling. I imagine that she took in everything, and the quiet reverence I've always read before may actually be a sense of "there are no words."

Her unspoken sentiment is: I can't begin to process nor share all that has happened for me.

---

What do you treasure?
What about this Christmas celebration do you need to keep to yourself?
What parts of your Christmas experience are worthy, edifying, and encouraging enough to share with others?

65

# WEEK 5, DAY 2

### *Dedicating*

*On the eighth day, when it was time to circumcise the child, he was named Jesus, the name the angel had given him before he was conceived. When the time came for the purification rites required by the Law of Moses, Joseph and Mary took him to Jerusalem to present him to the Lord (as it is written in the Law of the Lord, "Every firstborn male is to be consecrated to the Lord"), and to offer a sacrifice in keeping with what is said in the Law of the Lord: "a pair of doves or two young pigeons." – Luke 2: 21-24*

Mary and Joseph are following the Law of Moses. They are traditional Jews who are going through the proper ceremonies to bring their child before the Lord. Here again we see God turn the tradition upside down. This baby boy would traditionally be called Little Joe, but Mary and Joseph follow the angel's instructions and give Him the name Jesus.

It is ceremonial and foreshadowing as we see Mary and Joseph offer two birds as a sacrifice in honor of their son. Although they do not fully know now, their son will be the ultimate sacrifice to take away the sins of the world. Soon there will be no need for animal sacrifice.

Mary and Joseph again display that they are faithful Jews. They defy any ridicule they might encounter to bring their son before God and everyone to be dedicated back to God. It is not hard to imagine that they came in quietly and unassumingly. They may have wanted to remain unnoticed, as word may have spread to the perceived illegitimate nature of this baby. Mary and Joseph faithfully present themselves and their child for dedication in the temple. Then, as suddenly as the angels lit up the shepherds' sky, in the middle of their quiet little ritual, the silence is broken.

---

What does it look like to dedicate this year to God?
What verse or piece of scripture will you cling to when times get hard?
Who will know that your life is dedicated to serve the Living Lord?

67

# WEEK 5, DAY 3

### *Waiting Fulfilled*

*Now there was a man in Jerusalem called Simeon, who was righteous and devout. He was waiting for the consolation of Israel, and the Holy Spirit was on him. It had been revealed to him by the Holy Spirit that he would not die before he had seen the Lord's Messiah. Moved by the Spirit, he went into the temple courts. – Luke 2:25-27*

Simeon was a familiar face. He was like Norm in **Cheers** or the man who greets you every day at your local coffee shop. In the eighties, the sitcom **Cheers** memorialized the expression: "Hey Norm."

The fictitious Boston bar heralded itself a place "where everybody knows your name and they are always glad you came."

Simeon was like Norm. He was a man known for worshiping God and following God's law. Simeon believed that the Lord of Abraham, Isaac, and Jacob was going to redeem His people. It seems that Simeon was a frequent temple goer, though it doesn't say he was a priest. Simeon was a regular guy, whom the Holy Spirit had spoken to promising that he would see the Messiah before he died.

We can imagine that Simeon was old, that he was a teacher, and that everyone who shared space with him at the temple knew what the Holy Spirit had told him. Scripture says that the Holy Spirit nudged Simeon that day. You can almost imagine Simeon bustling in to the temple, wobbling on his cane but full of joy as he thought: "Today might be the day."

Everyone knew what Norm at **Cheers** was looking for when he arrived at the bar. Everyone knew what Simeon was looking for when he arrived at the temple. It wasn't tradition; it was familiar. Simeon enters the temple courts with hope and expectation. He is on high alert! He is looking for the King.

---

What is today the day for?
What has God told you to do?
Where is God calling you to walk?

# Week 5, Day 4

### *Holding God*

*Simeon took [Jesus] in his arms and praised God, saying: "Sovereign Lord, as you have promised, you may now dismiss your servant in peace. For my eyes have seen your salvation, which you have prepared in the sight of all nations: a light for revelation to the Gentiles and the glory of your people Israel." The child's father and mother marveled at what was said about him. Then Simeon blessed them and said to Mary, his mother: "This child is destined to cause the falling and rising of many in Israel, and to be a sign that will be spoken against, so that the thoughts of many hearts will be revealed. And a sword will pierce your own soul too." – Luke 2:28-35*

Simeon came to the temple that day wondering: "Is today the day?" He pushed through the crowds to see a young couple holding a baby boy. He walked up and grabbed the baby out of their arms. Then he talked to God. He muttered a prayer of thanksgiving and dismissal to the Lord of the Universe, saying: "You may now dismiss your servant in peace." The Prince of Peace, the little baby brings fulfillment to the prophesy of old and permission for Simeon to die.

Mary and Joseph must have been shocked. First this man they did not know grabbed their child and began to quote prophesy intertwined with his own eulogy. You don't get the sense that Mary reached back for the baby. There probably was little reaction time. Simeon blessed the parents and then turned to Mary. He said: "Your baby will be part of the fall and rise of Israel. He will reveal the truth in the hearts of the people—both good and bad. And finally your heart will be pierced in the process."

For Simeon this was the closest he has been to God. He shared a physical embrace with his Savior. Before Jesus sends the Holy Spirit, the Comforter, being at the temple was as close as people could get to God. Simeon's embrace of Jesus was the beginning of a beautiful fulfillment of the prophesy. He held God for an instant. We hold God in us all the time.

---

What would Jesus have to do for you, to release you in peace? How has He already been working in this way for you? When have you prayed for a peaceful release?

71

# WEEK 5, DAY 5

### *Finding Gratitude*

*There was also a prophetess, Anna, the daughter of Penuel, of the tribe of Asher. She was very old; she had lived with her husband seven years after her marriage, and then was a widow until she was eighty-four. She never left the temple but worshiped night and day, fasting and praying. Coming up to them at that very moment, she gave thanks to God and spoke about the child to all who were looking forward to the redemption of Jerusalem. – Luke 2:36-38*

Isn't it fitting that the story concludes with a woman? We began with Elizabeth's journey toward motherhood in her old age, and witnessed Mary's invitation to be the mother of God, and now our journey concludes with Anna, a prophetess who dedicated her widowhood to proclaim the coming King.

Anna notices Simeon's speech. She sees the baby lifted up above the on-lookers. She walks over with a sense of purpose. This is God in the flesh, the King she has waited for. She simply gives thanks and acknowledges that this baby is Him, the Messiah.

The Bible says that Anna is old. And with the conclusion of her story it says she spoke about the child to all who were looking forward to the fulfillment of the prophesy. She shared with anyone who would listened that the coming King had arrived. She spent the end of her days telling the story about her day in the temple when her wait ended and she saw the Messiah, Jesus.

---

What is gratitude?
What you grateful for?
How can you add a step of gratitude in your life this year?

73

# FINISHING WELL

*When Joseph and Mary had done everything required by the Law of the Lord, they returned to Galilee to their own town of Nazareth. And the child grew and became strong: he was filled with wisdom, and the grace of God was upon him. – Luke 2:39-40*

Another Christmas season has ended. You probably did a combination of things you wanted and things that were expected. Now, it's a new year, full of hope and promise.

Mary and Joseph left the big city and went back to their neighborhood. Joseph went back to carpentry and Mary cared for Jesus. After this extraordinary experience, they returned to ordinary life.

God desires to change us from ordinary to extraordinary. He longs to break with tradition and break into our lives. If you experienced God in a new or different way this Christmas, bring it into your everyday life.

Each of our Christmas cast of characters lived a life righteous in God's sight. Their life code was the Ten Commandments.

Consider writing the Ten Commandments in your own words. Refer to the Life Code on the next page for inspiration.

May the Christmas story change the way you do ordinary life.

# THE LIFE CODE

PUT **GOD** FIRST

**WORSHIP** ONLY GOD

**RESPECT** THE NAME OF GOD

**REST** ONE DAY A WEEK

**HONOR** YOUR PARENTS

REGARD LIFE AS **SACRED**

BE **FAITHFUL** IN MARRIAGE

**APPRECIATE** OTHER'S PROPERTY

ALWAYS BE **TRUTHFUL**

**CELEBRATE** OTHERS & THEIR BELONGINGS

# WRITE YOUR LIFE CODE

# Resources

**Scripture quotations from *The Holy Bible:***

New International Version®, NIV®, copyright © 1973, 1978, 1984, 2011 by Biblica, Inc.® Used by permission. All rights reserved worldwide.

New Living Translation, copyright © 1996, 2004, 2007 by Tyndale House Foundation. Used by permission of Tyndale House Publishers, Inc., Carol Stream, Illinois 60188. All rights reserved.

The Message, copyright © 1993, 1994, 1995, 1996, 2000, 2001, 2002. Used by permission of NavPress Publishing Group.

*Advent* begins on the fourth Sunday prior to Christmas Day (or the Sunday which falls closest to November 30th) in Western Christianity. In years when Christmas Eve falls on a Sunday, it is the last or fourth Sunday of Advent.

*The Lion King* © 1994 Walt Disney Pictures

*A Charlie Brown Christmas* © 1965 CBS (Columbia Broadcasting System)

*Luke for Everyone* © 2001, 2004 Nicholas Thomas Wright ISBN 978-0-281-05300-1

www.livingtheelijahproject.com © 2014, 2015 Andrea M. Polnaszek

*Definition of Joy:* Merriam-Webster Dictionary © 2015 Merriam-Webster, Incorporated

*Definition of Mercy:* Oxford Dictionary © 2015 Oxford University Press

*Cheers* (TV Series) 1982-1993 © Charles/Burrows/Charles Productions, Paramount Television

Life Code inspired by *Wish for Christmas* movie

Download additional resources:
www.andreapolnaszek.com

## *Jumping for Joy, pg 36*
### *Genesis 18:1-15, 21:1-7*
### The Three Visitors

*The Lord appeared to Abraham near the great trees of Mamre while he was sitting at the entrance to his tent in the heat of the day. Abraham looked up and saw three men standing nearby. When he saw them, he hurried from the entrance of his tent to meet them and bowed low to the ground.*

*He said, "If I have found favor in your eyes, my lord, do not pass your servant by. Let a little water be brought, and then you may all wash your feet and rest under this tree. Let me get you something to eat, so you can be refreshed and then go on your way–now that you have come to your servant."*

*"Very well," they answered, "do as you say."*

*So Abraham hurried into the tent to Sarah. "Quick," he said, "get three seahs of the finest flour and knead it and bake some bread."*

*Then he ran to the herd and selected a choice, tender calf and gave it to a servant, who hurried to prepare it. He then brought some curds and milk and the calf that had been prepared, and set these before them. While they ate, he stood near them under a tree.*

*"Where is your wife Sarah?" they asked him.*

*"There, in the tent," he said.*

*Then one of them said, "I will surely return to you about this time next year, and Sarah your wife will have a son."*

*Now Sarah was listening at the entrance to the tent, which was behind him. Abraham and Sarah were already very old, and Sarah was past the age of childbearing. So Sarah laughed to herself as she thought, "After I am worn out and my lord is old, will I now have this pleasure?"*

*Then the Lord said to Abraham, "Why did Sarah laugh and say, 'Will I really have a child, now that I am old?' Is anything too hard for the Lord? I will return to you at the appointed time next year, and Sarah will have a son."*

*Sarah was afraid, so she lied and said, "I did not laugh."*

*But he said, "Yes, you did laugh."*

### The Birth of Isaac

*Now the Lord was gracious to Sarah as he had said, and the Lord did for Sarah what he had promised. Sarah became pregnant and bore a son to Abraham in his old age, at the very* time God had promised him. Abraham gave the name Isaac to the son Sarah bore him. When his son Isaac was eight days old, Abraham circumcised him, as God commanded him. Abraham was a hundred years old when his son Isaac was born to him.

Sarah said, "God has brought me laughter, and everyone who hears about this will laugh with me." And she added, "Who would have said to Abraham that Sarah would nurse children? Yet I have borne him a son in his old age."

## Meditation: Joy, pg 33
## Meditation: Peace, pg 61

### Matthew 2:1-12
### The Magi Visit the Messiah

After Jesus was born in Bethlehem in Judea, during the time of King Herod, Magi from the east came to Jerusalem and asked, "Where is the one who has been born king of the Jews? We saw his star when it rose and have come to worship him."

When King Herod heard this he was disturbed, and all Jerusalem with him. When he had called together all the people's chief priests and teachers of the law, he asked them where the Messiah was to be born. "In Bethlehem in Judea," they replied, "for this is what the prophet has written:

> "'But you, Bethlehem, in the land of Judah,
> are by no means least among the rulers of Judah;
> for out of you will come a ruler
> who will shepherd my people Israel.'"

Then Herod called the Magi secretly and found out from them the exact time the star had appeared. He sent them to Bethlehem and said, "Go and search carefully for the child. As soon as you find him, report to me, so that I too may go and worship him."

After they had heard the king, they went on their way, and the star they had seen when it rose went ahead of them until it stopped over the place where the child was. When they saw the star, they were overjoyed. On coming to the house, they saw the child with his mother Mary, and they bowed down and worshiped him. Then they opened their treasures and *presented him with gifts of gold, frankincense and myrrh. And having been warned in a dream not to go back to Herod, they returned to their country by another route.*

---

## Breaking Light Into Dark, pg 50

### Psalm 23
### A psalm of David.

*The Lord is my shepherd, I lack nothing.
He makes me lie down in green pastures,
he leads me beside quiet waters,
he refreshes my soul.
He guides me along the right paths
for his name's sake.
Even though I walk
through the darkest valley,
I will fear no evil,
for you are with me;
your rod and your staff,
they comfort me.
You prepare a table before me
in the presence of my enemies.
You anoint my head with oil;
my cup overflows.
Surely your goodness and love will follow me
all the days of my life,
and I will dwell in the house of the Lord
forever.*

---

## Obeying the Song, pg 58

### 1 Samuel 17:34-36

*But David said to Saul, "Your servant has been keeping his father's sheep. When a lion or a bear came and carried off a sheep from the flock, I went after it, struck it and rescued the sheep from its mouth. When it turned on me, I seized it by its hair, struck it and killed it. Your servant has killed both the lion and the bear; this uncircumcised Philistine will be like one of them, because he has defied the armies of the living God."*

For more information and resources by the author:

**WWW.ANDREAPOLNASZEK.COM**

Made in the USA
Columbia, SC
30 November 2023